'The author is a comparative newcomer to children's books; on this evidence, he should go far.'

'A handsome creation.'

'Perfect for newly developing readers and great to share.'

'Watch out for this new kid on the children's books block, you will be won over!'

'I loved everything about this book.'

468 971 04 0

For Georgia,
the girl with the dancing feet.

Text and illustrations copyright © 2013 Alex T. Smith
First published in Great Britain in 2013 by Hodder Children's Books

The right of Alex T. Smith to be identified as the Author and Illustrator
of this Work has been asserted by him in accordance with the Copyright,
Designs and Patents Act 1988.

FIRST EDITION

10 9 8 7 6 5 4 3 2 1

A catalogue record for this book is available from the British Library

978 1 444 90929 6

Design by Alison Still

Printed and bound in China

The paper and board used in this paperback by Hodder Children's Books
are natural recyclable products made from wood grown in sustainable forests.
The manufacturing processes conform to the environmental regulations of
the country of origin.

Hodder Children's Books
a division of Hachette Children's Books
338 Euston Road, London NW1 3BH
www.hachette.co.uk

CLAUDE

in the Spotlight

ALEX T. SMITH

Behind a red front door with
a big brass knocker, lives a
little dog named Claude.

And here he is!

hello !

4

Fancy red beret

stylish red sweater

well polished shoes

Claude is a small dog.
Claude is a small, plump dog.
Claude is a small, plump dog
who wears a fancy red beret
and a stylish red sweater.

Claude's owners are Mr and Mrs Shinyshoes and his best friend is Sir Bobblysock.

Sir Bobblysock is both a sock and quite bobbly.

Every morning, Mr and Mrs
Shinyshoes wave goodbye to Claude
and set off for work. And that is
when the fun begins. Where will
Claude and Sir Bobblysock go today?

One day, shortly after Mr and Mrs Shinyshoes had skedaddled out of the door, Claude leapt out of bed with a spring in his step, dislodging Sir Bobblysock's hairnet and almost knocking over his cup of tea.

Claude should have been feeling
rather sleepy because the night
before he had stayed up VERY
late (until about half past eight)
reading a book of ghost stories.

Some of the ghosts were very spooky looking. Claude was especially worried about how they floated about and didn't wear any shoes…

11

But that was last night.
Now Claude was wide awake
with his beret on, looking for
something to do.

'I think I will go for a walk
into town,' he said, so he did.

Sir Bobblysock decided to go too. Really his hair wanted washing, but he felt that no good would come of him lounging about all day with his head wrapped up in a towel, so the two friends set off.

13

Suddenly, a troupe of
children walked by.

They seemed to be wearing
some very funny outfits.
Very funny indeed…

Claude's nose tingled, his eyebrows wiggled, and behind him his bottom started to wag his tail. There was DEFINITELY an adventure brewing here!

Quickly smoothing down his ears, Claude ran after the children with Sir Bobblysock hopping along behind.

They followed the children
into a big, bright room. The
wall on one side was completely
covered by a mirror. There was
a tall upright piano in one
corner and an old lady sitting
at it, playing a very jolly tune.

Claude was just about to ask if
he could play a little ditty, when
the classroom door flew open.

Into the room leapt an extraordinary looking woman!

'Good morning, everybody!' the lady boomed. 'My name is Miss Henrietta Highkick-Spin, and I'm your teacher. Now come along, everyone, let's daaaaance!'

It all looked a bit too much for Sir Bobblysock who had his knees to consider, so he went and lay on the top of the piano.

'First,' called Miss Highkick-Spin,
'we must warm up our bodies!'
and she began skipping about and
doing all sorts of strange stretches.

Claude found the skipping very
easy indeed and he enjoyed the
breeze around his ears as he
galloped across the room.

The stretches, however, were
a different matter.

Claude found that his tummy
got in the way…

After everyone was nice and warm,
Miss Highkick-Spin taught the
class a nice gentle dance routine.

There was some more skipping about, some leg waggling, and some 'waving-your-arms-above-your-head-and-pretending-you-are-a-daisy-in-a-windy-meadow'.

Claude tried really hard to join in, but when it came to the arm waving his paws got knotted in his ears.

'Don't worry,' said Miss Highkick-Spin, 'Ballet's not for everyone. Let's try some tap!' And she handed Claude some exciting new shoes.

Claude put them on and thought he looked lovely. When he walked they made a wonderful TAP TAP TAP noise on the floor. He showed them to Sir Bobblysock who said they were great, but that he felt one of his heads coming on.

Miss Highkick-Spin was just about to teach the class a noisy new dance when something happened...

A tiny fly, who had seen Claude waving his arms above his head and pretending to be a daisy in a windy meadow...

...went up Claude's jumper!

27

Claude couldn't help himself.
It tickled.

He skittered and
jittered across the room.

He leapt and dived
high up into the air.

He wiggled and
jiggled all over until
he was almost a blur.

Sir Bobblysock
needed a big cup
of tea from just
looking at him.

29

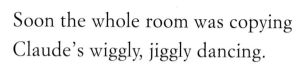

Soon the whole room was copying
Claude's wiggly, jiggly dancing.
Even the old lady joined in
with the leg kicking and
bottom shaking!

Eventually the fly got a bit bored, escaped from Claude's jumper and disappeared out of the window.

Claude came to a standstill.

'Phew!' panted the dance teacher, pink in the face. 'What a wonderful new dance! You MUST join us in the show we are performing in at the theatre this afternoon! Do say you will?'

Claude didn't like to ask what a theatre was, so he just smoothed his jumper over his tummy and nodded politely.

About an hour later, after the children had eaten their packed lunches and Claude and Sir Bobblysock had tucked into the emergency picnic that Claude always kept under his beret, the whole class set off for the theatre.

THEATRE

This Afternoon Only!
The VARIETY SHOW
AMAZING ACTS! DARING FEATS!
WORLD FAMOUS PERFORMERS!
AND A SPECIAL
GRAND PRIZE!

On the way, one of the girls explained to Claude all about the show they would soon be starring in. It was going to be a variety show.

'That means lots of different people do different things on the stage,' said the girl. 'We will be doing your new dance! And the most exciting thing is that today, the best act wins a grand prize – all the cakes you can eat from Mr Lovelybuns' Bakery. He's judging the competition.'

Claude clapped his paws together
and Sir Bobblysock let out a sigh.

Mr Lovelybuns' Bakery was
Claude's favourite shop. Even
Sir Bobblysock, who could be
quite picky with his pastries, had
declared that Mr Lovelybuns had
the nicest buns he'd ever seen.

Unfortunately, in the
excitement, nobody
saw a suspicious looking
man listening in on
their conversation...

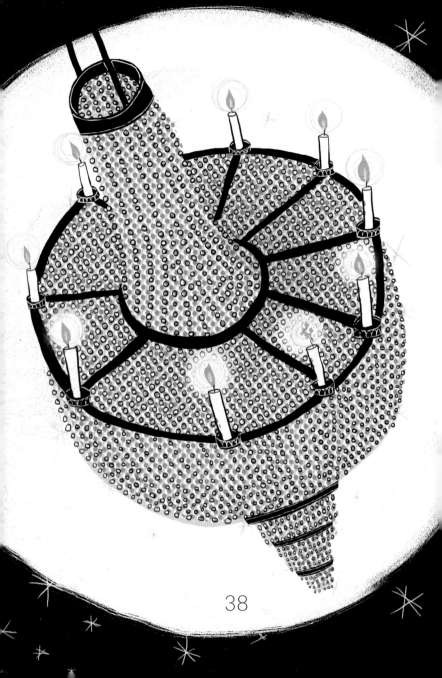

Claude and Sir Bobblysock liked the theatre immediately. Sir Bobblysock liked the glitz and glamour of the whole place.

High above the audience's seats was a big, sparkly chandelier. Sir Bobblysock said that you wouldn't want that falling on your head. Claude nodded his head in agreement, then everyone trouped off backstage.

39

Claude couldn't believe how different it was. It was dark and dusty and rather spooky.

'This is just the sort of place a ghost would live,' shivered Claude, remembering his book of ghosties at home.

HAS ANYONE SEEN MY TROUSERS?
THE CLASSIC TRAGEDY
starring Sidney Thomas
* * * * *

BILLY BONGO
in
Who's Afraid of Virginia Woof?
* * * * * * * * * *

Harriet J. Harmon
in
THE SMASH HIT
Hello SAILORS!
* * * * *

THE INTERNATIONALLY ACCLAIMED MUSICAL
PUSSYCATS
starring Corinne Golch
LIMITED RUN! BOOK NOW!

1.

THE DANCE DIVA'S DANCE TROUPE

And he and Sir Bobblysock quickly hurried along to the brightly lit dressing rooms.

41

In the first room they found a
troupe of ladies who would be
doing a dance routine, too. Sir
Bobblysock couldn't take his eyes
off the ladies' extraordinary costumes.

In the next room was The Marvellous Marvin, a magician.

Claude and Sir Bobblysock watched in amazement as he waggled his magic wand about and produced three tiny rabbits from his hat.

44

Then Claude had a go…

In the final dressing
room was an
enormous woman
dressed as a viking.

Her special trick was singing – so high and so loud that she could shatter a teacup. Claude and Sir Bobblysock put on the safety goggles that Claude always kept under his beret and watched as the viking demonstrated with her teacup.

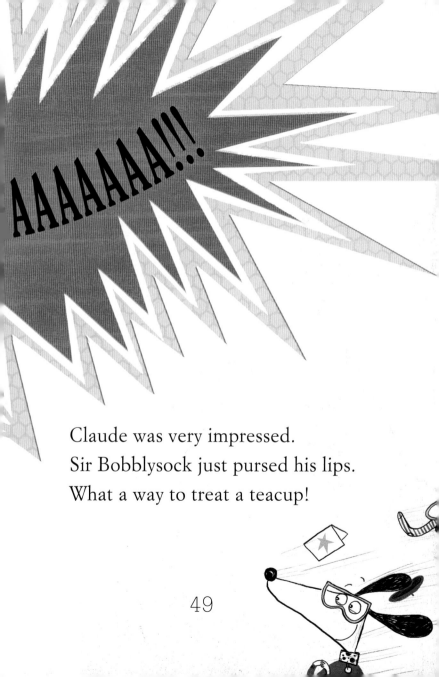

AAAAAAA!!!

Claude was very impressed.
Sir Bobblysock just pursed his lips.
What a way to treat a teacup!

49

Of course, Claude couldn't wait to
have a go, but as hard as he tried,
the glass vase wouldn't budge.

Eventually Sir Bobblysock slyly
elbowed it off the table...

Claude was just enjoying a pre-show
biscuit when there came a shout
from down the corridor...

The Marvellous Marvin
was standing in front
of the dressing room
looking very pale.

52

'A g-g-g-ghost just jumped out at me
and tried to snatch my magic wand,'
he said shakily. 'It's broken, look!'

He held up the wand.
It was all bent and
limp like a sad sock.

'The Theatre Ghost!' said Miss. Highkick-Spin dramatically. 'Every theatre has a ghost, but I've never heard of one behaving so badly before.'

Claude shivered. He would have
to keep his eyes peeled for this
ghost. It was clearly trouble with
a capital T. Sir Bobblysock
couldn't stop his bobbles from
shaking. All this talk of ghosts
had given him the collywobbles.

Before anyone could say any
more, a man with a clipboard
bustled through the crowd.

'Places please, everyone!' he said.
'The show is about to begin!'

Claude and Sir Bobblysock rushed
to the side of the stage to watch.

But first, they couldn't help
popping their heads through
the plush red curtains to
look at the audience.

Directly underneath
the big chandelier
was Mr Lovelybuns.

He was sitting at a special judging table and looked very important. Claude waved and Mr Lovelybuns waved back.

Suddenly the orchestra started up and the show began.

The dancing ladies were halfway through their hot shoe shuffle when the ghost leapt out from the darkness and terrified them. One by one, they all fell over.

The last dancer tumbled head first
into the orchestra pit and got
her head stuck
in a tuba.

The Marvellous Marvin was no better. His wonky wand didn't work at all. Instead of making a big puff of smoke come out of his hat, he set it on fire. Claude had to rush onto the stage with his beret full of water to put it out.

The audience groaned. The show was an absolute disaster!

Soon it was Claude's turn to take to the stage. Sir Bobblysock watched from the wings.

Claude shuffled on
with the other dancers
and when the music
started, he nervously
wiggled and jiggled about.

All of a sudden, Claude heard the stomping of shoes behind him.

He spun around on the spot
and there was the ghost!

Miss Highkick-Spin screamed.
The children squealed
and everyone hotfooted
it into the wings.

Claude joined Sir Bobblysock backstage and Sir Bobblysock hid up Claude's jumper. He was all of a quiver and desperately needed one of his long lie downs.

'Something isn't quite right here,' thought Claude, and he thought so hard that his head started to hurt.

The viking was the next act. She had already smashed a tumbler and a crystal statue of a poodle when Claude saw the ghost tiptoe onto the stage behind her.

Claude looked at the ghost –
from the top of its white head
to the bottom of its shoes.

69

That was it!
Claude wagged his
tail. None of the ghosts in his
book at home wore shoes – especially
not great galumphing ones like that.
They *floated* daintily about, shoeless.

So if this ghost was wearing shoes,
it couldn't be a real ghost at all.

Claude ran onto the stage.

'This isn't a ghostie!' he cried.
'It is a very naughty person indeed.'

And he grabbed the ghost's
white sheet and pulled it off.
Underneath was a shifty-
looking man. His face
was very red and he
looked down at
the floor.

Everybody gasped
like this: *GASP!*

'What on earth are you up to, you naughty man?' said Claude

Sir Bobblysock hopped out from Claude's jumper and put his specs on so he could get a better look at the action.

'I just LOVE cakes,' said the naughty man, 'and when I heard someone telling you that the grand prize was all the cakes you could eat, I wanted to win them. Only, I'm not very good at anything…'

The audience said 'Aaaaaaaaah' sadly.

'So I thought if I could stop everyone else from winning, I could come on and do anything and win the competition...'

The audience said 'Oooooooh' crossly.

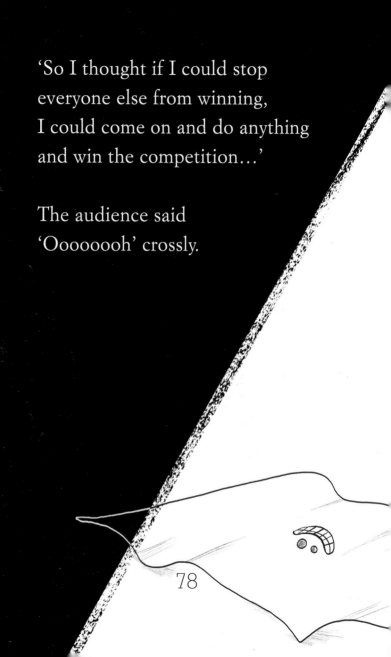

'So I went to Ida Down's Bed Emporium and bought myself this sheet and…'

Claude was just going to wag his finger at the naughty man, when –

CREAK! GROAN!

Mr Lovelybuns let out a yelp!
The big chandelier above his head
looked like it was about to fall.
The viking's scream must have
set it off. If Mr Lovelybuns didn't
move, the whole thing would
crash down on his head!

Everybody watched as the
chandelier swayed. Then all
of a sudden it started to fall!

Everyone panicked.
Everyone except Claude.

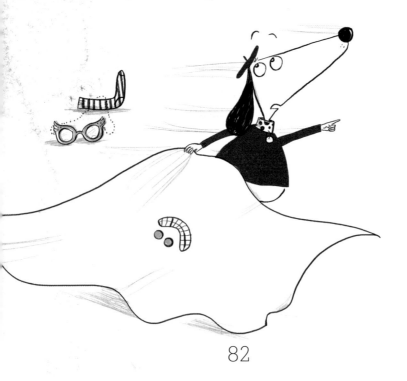

'Quick!' cried Claude to
the naughty man and they
ran over to Mr Lovelybuns.

Sir Bobblysock had a dizzy fit
and fell over with a swoon.

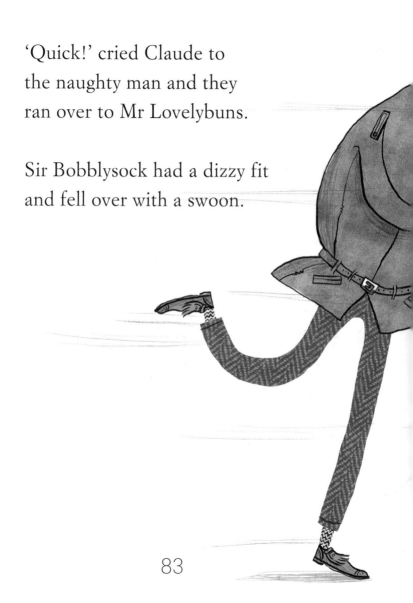

Claude and the naughty man stretched out the ghost's white sheet just in time and...

...caught the chandelier!

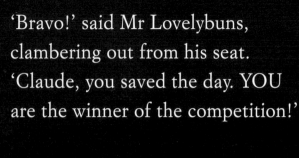

'Bravo!' said Mr Lovelybuns, clambering out from his seat. 'Claude, you saved the day. YOU are the winner of the competition!'

Everybody in the theatre clapped and some even threw flowers. Claude blushed and shyly shook Mr Lovelybuns' hand. Sir Bobbysock moved to the side on account of his hay fever.

Miss Highkick-Spin fought
her way through the crowds.

'Claude,' she said, with tears
in her eyes. 'You are the most
wonderful dancer I've ever seen.
Won't you and Sir Bobblysock
come and travel the world with
me and dance in theatres all
over the place?'

Claude thought about
it for a moment.

Now that he'd got the hang of it,
he did rather enjoy dancing and
shaking his bottom about. But
then he did love
living at Mr and
Mrs Shinyshoes'
house too.

He looked at Sir Bobblysock.
He was as white as a sheet and
looked like he had seen a hundred
ghosts. What he needed was one
of his long lie downs with a cup
of tea and a cream horn.

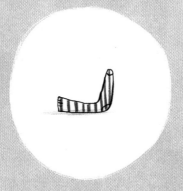

Claude politely explained all of this to Miss Highkick-Spin who understood.

Then, after saying goodbye to everyone, Claude and Sir Bobblysock made their way home, only stopping to call into Mr Lovelybuns' Bakery.

Later that day, when Mr and Mrs Shinyshoes came home from work, they were surprised to find their kitchen full of cakes and pastries.

'Where on earth have all these cakes come from?' said Mrs Shinyshoes. 'Do you think Claude knows anything about them?'

Mr Shinyshoes laughed. 'Don't be silly – look, he's been fast asleep all day!'

But of course Claude DID know
where all the cakes had come from.

94

And we do too, don't we?

How to Spot a Ghost:

Is it wearing shoes?
(If so, it isn't a ghost.)

Is it floating about?
(If so, it *might* be a ghost.)

Is it just a naughty person wearing a bed sheet?

(If so, it *probably* isn't a ghost.)

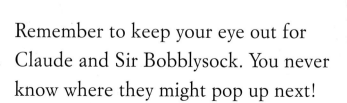

Remember to keep your eye out for Claude and Sir Bobblysock. You never know where they might pop up next!